MY GRANDPA IS AMAZING

Nick Butterworth

WALKER BOOKS

AND SUBSIDIARIES

LONDON • BOSTON • SYDNEY

My grandpa is amazing.

He builds fantastic
sand-castles …

and he makes
marvellous drinks ...

and he's
not at all afraid
of heights ...

and he makes
wonderful flower
arrangements ...

and he's a
brilliant driver ...

and he knows
all about first aid ...

and he's got an amazing bike ...

and he's a
terrific dancer ...

and he's very, very,
very patient ...

and he invents
brilliant games.

It's great to have a
grandpa like mine.

He's amazing!

NICK BUTTERWORTH says of **My Grandpa Is Amazing**, "I wonder how much time I spent as a boy singing the praises of my family. My grandpa could make *anything* out of *anything*. My gran was the best friend anyone could ever wish for. My dad was little short of Superman and my mum ... well, perhaps she actually *was* Wonderwoman! It's heartening to know that children feel the same today as I did then. Especially my own two!"

Nick Butterworth has worked as a graphic designer, television presenter, magazine editor and cartoon-strip illustrator, and has written and illustrated many successful children's books as well. These include the Walker titles *My Dad Is Brilliant*, *My Mum Is Fantastic*, *My Grandma Is Wonderful*, *Making Faces*, *Jack the Carpenter and His Friends* and *Jill the Farmer and Her Friends*. Nick is also the creator of the bestselling *Percy the Park Keeper* series.

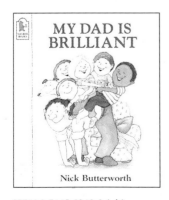

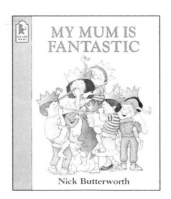

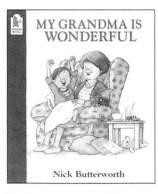

ISBN 0-7445-8248-2 (pb)   ISBN 0-7445-8249-0 (pb)   ISBN 0-7445-8251-2 (pb)

First published 1991 by Walker Books Ltd
87 Vauxhall Walk, London SE11 5HJ

This edition published 2001

2 4 6 8 10 9 7 5 3 1

© 1991 Nick Butterworth

This book has been typeset in Times

Printed in Hong Kong

British Library Cataloguing in Publication Data:
a catalogue record for this book is available from the British Library

ISBN 0-7445-8250-4

THIS WALKER BOOK BELONGS TO: